AM I YOURS?

Alex Latimer

Published by
PEACHTREE PUBLISHERS
1700 Chattahoochee Avenue
Atlanta, Georgia 30318-2112
www.peachtree-online.com

Text and illustrations © 2018 by Alex Latimer

First published in Great Britain in 2018 by Oxford University Press
First United States version published in 2018 by Peachtree Publishers

The illustrations were created as pencil drawings, digitized, then finished with color and texture.

Printed in China
10 9 8 7 6 5 4 3 2 1
First Edition

ISBN 978-1-68263-044-0

Library of Congress Cataloging-in-Publication Data

Names: Latimer, Alex, author, illustrator.
Title: Am I yours? / Alex Latimer.
Description: First edition. | Atlanta : Peachtree Publishers, 2018. | Summary: "Some friendly dinosaurs must help a lost egg
after it's blown out of its nest. But if they are to reunite the little egg with its true parents,
they must first discover what kind of dinosaur lies inside"— Provided by publisher.
Identifiers: LCCN 2017040315 | ISBN 9781682630440
Subjects: | CYAC: Identity—Fiction. | Eggs—Fiction. | Lost children—Fiction. | Dinosaurs—Fiction.
Classification: LCC PZ8.3.L34445 Am 2018 | DDC [E]—dc23 LC record available at https://lccn.loc.gov/2017040315

Paper used in the production of this book is a natural, recyclable product made
from wood grown in sustainable forests. The manufacturing process conforms
to the environmental regulations of the country of origin.

AM I YOURS?

Alex Latimer

PEACHTREE
ATLANTA

Two hundred million years ago
an icy wind began to blow.
It blew great clouds from east to west
and pushed an egg out of a nest.

The egg rolled gently down a hill,
slow at first, then fast, until—

it bumped a rock and spun around
and came to land on level ground.

It sat there through that cold, dark night.
At last it felt the warm sunlight.
And with the light came thumping feet.
The egg called out, soft and sweet:

"Excuse me, please,
but am I yours?
I'm sure I am
a dinosaur's!"

First, Stegosaurus wandered near
and asked the egg, loud and clear:
"What do you look like inside that shell?
I can't see in so I can't tell.
Are there spikes along your spine?
Long and flat and sharp like mine?"

"I have no spikes, I'm sad to say.
So I'm not yours, but that's okay."

Next, Brachiosaurus leaned in low
and asked his questions, calm and slow:
"What do you look like inside that shell?
I can't see in so I can't tell.
Do you have a longish neck?
Or is it short? Can you check?"

"It's very short, this neck of mine.
So I'm not yours, but I'll be fine."

Triceratops came trotting by
and spoke to the egg, eye to eye:
"What do you look like inside that shell?
I can't see in so I can't tell.
Do you have horns—one, two, and three?
Three sharp horns, just like me?"

"I have no horns—I wish I did!—
so I'm not yours. I'm not your kid."

Corythosaurus ambled past.
She stopped and stared, then spoke at last:
"What do you look like inside that shell?
I can't see in so I can't tell.
Is there a crest upon your head?
Or is it flat and smooth instead?"

"I have no crest (I just checked now) so I'm not yours. Thanks, anyhow."

Tyrannosaurus came to see
and asked the egg, quite lovingly:
"What do you look like inside that shell?
I can't see in so I can't tell.
Do you have a mouth of teeth?
Sharp up top and down beneath?"

"My teeth are few," the egg replied.
"So I'm not yours," it said and sighed.

The sun sank slowly in the sky
and the lonely egg began to cry . . .

"The light of day is fading fast.
I'm sure this night will be my last!
I can't survive in wind and storm!
I'll freeze alone! I must stay warm!"

"You are not ours, whose could you be?
We wish there was a way to see."

But as the sun began to set,
it showed a perfect silhouette . . .

A pair of wings, a pointy snout.
And two strong legs, both short and stout.

"We see you now inside your shell!
We know your folks!
We know them well!"

The egg was rolled back up the hill,
rolled and nudged and pushed until
they reached a soft and sandy mound.
They left it where it would be found.

Then came the thump of heavy feet.
The egg called out, so soft and sweet . . .

"One last time—I must be sure—
Are you the ones I'm looking for?"

"We are. We are! We are YOURS!
We're two ECSTATIC pterosaurs."

And when the night had come and gone—
the sky was clear with the light of dawn—
there came a tap! A crack and scratch!
And the lucky egg began to hatch.

DEINOSUCHUS

PARAPUZOSIA

DIMETRODON

RHINOREX

CORYTHOSAURUS

DIPLODOCUS

PACHYCEPHALOSAURUS

AMARGASAURUS

DESMATOSUCHUS

PTEROSAUR

PLOTOSAURUS

TRICERATOPS

COELOPHYSIS

MIRAGAIA

CAMEROCERAS